Sorry Dear

Sorry Dear

A SCREENPLAY BY

AJAY RAMPHUL

Primix Publishing
East Brunswick Office Evolution
1 Tower Center Boulevard, Ste 1510
East Brunswick, NJ 08816
www.primixpublishing.com
Phone: 1-800-538-5788

Published by Primix Publishing: 01/09/2024

ISBN: 979-8-89194-367-4(sc)
ISBN: 979-8-89194-368-1(e)

Library of Congress Control Number: 2024922046

SCENE 1

EXT SHOT: IN THE STREETS – DURING THE DAY

ENTER: FELIX, RAM, MEERA, SUNIL, TOMMY AND HIS GOONS

FELIX (a quiet old man) and his men, armed with guns, are tailing a car. MEERA, 22, a beautiful young woman with grey-blue eyes, is taking pictures of the views around her. TOMMY, one of Felix's men, spots her. Tommy then decides to follow her, accompanied by another GOON. Having noticed that Tommy and his goon are after her, Meera starts walking fast in the streets.

Meera, visibly frightened, quickens her pace. As her fear mounts, she breaks into a run, only to collide with a man and tumble to the ground. The man, RAM, a striking figure, is instantly drawn to her. He rushed to her aid, his protective instincts kicking in as he gazes int her eyes, brimming with emotion and concern.

MEERA (Desperately)

Help me, help me, please!

Ram looks unceasingly at Meera.

RAM (Smiling reassuringly)

Don't worry, my beauty! Stay here! You are safe with me,

baby! They do not know the power of Ram. (Flaunting
his biceps to Meera in a body-building pose)

Meera smiles back at Ram and replies positively.

MEERA

No need to worry about the demons if God is by my side. My Hero!

RAM

Yes lovely. Ram is by your side. Stay here
and watch how I deliver you.

Furious, Ram turns his attention to the goons, removes his gun, and runs towards them. Ram stops them.

RAM (Defiantly)

Hey you. Why are you worrying this beautiful lady?

One of the goons answers.

GOON 1 (Dismissively)

This is none of your business. Step aside. Go home.

RAM (Threateningly)

Leave that girl alone. Otherwise....

GOON 2 (mocking)

Otherwise.... What?

Ram runs towards them and jumps in the air with his right foot stretched. He hits one of the goons directly on this cheeks. Three of his teeth flies in the air and he falls down. All of the other goons are astonished with Ram's agility and power. They look at each other and after some seconds of hesitation they all run towards Ram. A vigorous fight starts.

At the same moment a guy named SUNIL, aged 25, is passing by and witnesses the fight.

On the other hand, watches the prowess of Ram. But she is too frightened. She sees a taxi coming, stops it and rapidly jumps into it in muted silence.

MEERA (Frantic)

Despite her urgency, Sunil is captivated by the fight, a smile playing on his lips as he watches intently.

SUNIL (Thinking, smiling in this thoughts)

Hmm, I was looking for a fighter friend, and he is in
front of me! God knows where to send his servant.

The goons are no match for Ram, who effortlessly dispatches them with a series of well-placed blows.

SUNIL (Talking to himself)

Okay! Give blow! One! Two! Three! Yeah, that's it, my action
hero! You are the one I have been looking for since so long.

Sunil, thoroughly engrossed, cheers on the sideline. His excitement peaks.

SUNIL

This is a live street fight show.

In a moment of excitement, Sunil punches a wooden panel, immediately regretting it as pain shoots through his hand. He yelps.

SUNIL

Ouch! …

Staggering from the pain, he makes a few rounds and falls heavily onto the ground.

Ram, after beating the goons black and blue, hurries back to Sunil, concerned.

RAM (quickly)

Hey dude, are you alright?

SUNIL (Groggy)

Oh yes. I am fine, bro. Say, you are a real iron man.

RAM

Oh no, my friend. That's too much. But I try to keep
the form. I do workouts every day. See that.

Ram flexes, showing off his biceps, which Sunil admires with a nod. Sunil touches his biceps.

SUNIL

As I said, a real iron man.

RAM

Okay, leave that. Have you noticed that beautiful girl
with grey-blue eyes? I told her to wait for me here. I
can't see her. I don't know where she has gone.

Sunil is initially stunned, not remembering any. He is taken aback by Ram's question about the girl.

SUNIL (Thinking)

'About whom is he talking? I didn't notice any girl!'

RAM (Worriedly)

'Hey, tell me! Did you see that girl? I have
not been able to talk to her, man!'

SUNIL

'Oh yes, yes! That girl, I saw her. Such an
incredible beauty! Really an Angel!'

Sunil, always the prankster, decides to play along.

SUNIL (Thinking to himself, mischievously)

I will fool you, Ram, as you seem so desperate to find your girl.

TALKING BY SIGN

They exchange phone numbers through hand gestures, mischievously
plotting.

RAM

Take my mobile number, man! … You call
me when you see her somewhere.

SUNIL

OK! Let me save the number, man!

RAM

Ok. I need to go. Don't forget to call anytime you sees her.

SUNIL

Count on me, bro. Bye. See you soon.

Ram takes his bicycle and rides away. Once alone, Sunil reveals his
true thoughts.

Sunil laughs obtrusively.

                    SUNIL (Talking to himself)

I didn't even see her, man! If I had seen such a gorgeous girl
with grey-blue eyes, I would be hitting on her myself, dude!

Sunil's laughter fills the air as he regains his composure and continues
on his way.

CUT TO:

SCENE 2

EXT SHOT: BEACH

SUNNY DAY, The sun beats down on a picturesque beach. Waves crash gently in the background.

ENTER: ANNY, BILL AND SUNIL

Sunil approaches, leisurely strolling, then stops to observe a young couple, ANNY and BILL, girlfriend making a toast. They seem really happy together, cheering for a special occasion. He sits down under a shade and observes them for a while. Suddenly, the mood shifts. He comes closer to see what's happening. Bill is consuming too much alcohol, becoming excessively drunk. He is really sour. Sunil edges closer, curiously eavesdrops on their argument. They are having a dispute, and the Bill is scolding Anny.

SUNIL (Muttering to himself)

This couple is so weird! A few minutes ago, they were

on good terms, celebrating together, showing love and affection
to each other, and now they are yelling at each other…ha,
ha, ha! That's why, wise men say: Never Fall in Love!!!

Anny confronts Bill about his drinking

ANNY

I have told you to stop drinking right now,
Bill! You are already tanked up!

BILL (Slurring, defiant)

Oh, Anny, please! Let me be! I told you before not to interfere when
I drink alcohol! Just don't bother about me, okay. I love drinking.

ANNY

Bill, you look like a drunken bull!

Anny reproaches him further leading to Bill to pushes her away in a
drunken stupor.

BILL (Angry)

Just leave me alone and get lost!

Anny is distraught, and Bill's behaviour really saddens her, but she then
decides to take a stand against Bill's drinking problem.

ANNY

Look, Bill! Stop it now, and let's go home.
Otherwise, I will leave you forever!

BILL (Bitterly)

Well, it will be good for me, isn't it? At least I can
live my life in peace. Go to hell, you witch!

Anny is both hurt and angry at the same time.

ANNY (Sadly, deeply hurt)

Your harsh words can break my heart. Love can be so painful.

ANNY (Through her tears)

Fine, you looked for it! So now, never call me again. Goodbye!

BILL

Goodbye. Good riddance.

Enraged, Anny leaves. It was then that Bill noticed there were no bottles left.

BILL (Talking to himself)

What a fool I am. I should have asked her to buy some bottles before telling her to leave. What am I going to do now?

On the other side, Sunil sees left over bottles in the dump. He has an idea. He approaches Bill to give him company.

SUNIL

Hello, buddy! How are you? What's your name? Want more?

Bill eagerly accepts, unaware of Suni's intentions.

BILL (Willingly)

I am okay! My name is Bill! Yes, of course, buddy! Not even one drop left!

SUNIL

Okay, wait for me here! I will see what I can do. I will be right back!

BILL

Be quick! I can't wait anymore!

Far away, Sunil finds some leftover rum in a bottle and wasted fried chicken bones in the dump. He takes the rum bottle to Bill cautiously with a great smile on his face and mischief in his eyes. Bill is unaware of what's going to happen next!

BILL

'Oh, thanks, bro! Really, you're a true brother!'

As soon as Sunil is about to give Bill the bottle, he suddenly stops.

SUNIL (Teasing)

Hmmm…to begin with, give me Rs1!

BILL

What! But I don't have that money with me right now!

SUNIL

Okay, 50 cents then?

BILL (Loudly, desperately)

I have nothing! I just want to drink! Please! I
beg of you! Let me have a sip, please!

SUNIL

No money, no drink!

Sunil is infuriating him.

BILL (Furiously)

Give that to me. you scoundrel! Give it to
me right now!'

SUNIL (Laughing)

You will get nothing, my friend.

Bill starts using vulgar language.

BILL

You mother fu...

Hearing that, Sunil moves away. Bill stands up to stop him, but due to his drunkenness, he falls down heavily. Sunil sees a rope not far away. He picks it up. He ties Bill's arms with his body and feet. Bill moves like a zombie and sometimes jumps like a wounded corpse.

Since he is tied up, he does not watch his steps and falls into a tiny pit that has recently been dug by children. Witnessing the weird behaviour and unnatural incident, the kids flee away with fear. This awesome entertainment induces Sunil to burst out in laughter.

SUNIL

Bill, you are not fully covered with grey sand!
Let me help you! It is a bit muddy!

Sunil covers him properly with sand up to his neck. Owing to the fact that Bill is heavily drunk, he cannot control himself. Sunil looks at a few stray dogs near the dumps and laughs loudly.

SUNIL (With a burst of laughter)

Are you famished, buddy?

SUNIL (Pondering to himself)

Oh, you want food, wait! Delicious hot food from the hotel…

Sunil returns to the dumps. To his dismay, he finds more aggressive, hungry stray dogs searching for food and growling at each other. Seeing that, Sunil picks up some dead corals, rocks, and flings and shoves them.

The latter frighteningly takes the few chicken bones and makes the dogs sniff them.

SUNIL (Commanding with a smirk)

Go! Go! Bark or bite him.

He heads toward Bill.

SUNIL (Obtrusively)

Bill, I've got hot and crispy fried chicken for you! They
seem to be very tasty. I am sure you will like them.

BILL (Beaming with hope, smiling)

Please bring them to me quickly! I'm starving.

Eagerly, Sunil advances as the dogs bark in the background. Suddenly,
he sprints ahead and tosses the bones onto Bill. The stray dogs, now
fixated on Bill, clamber onto him, barking and scrambling for the
bones. Caught in a predicament, Bill's screams as echo as he seeks a
way out from his helpless state.

CUT TO:

SUNIL (Thinking)

But where is the princess?

Sunil looks around anxiously and notices Anny behind a tree. She
laughs silently and watches the action thoroughly. Sunil walks gallantly
and goes to her.

SUNIL

Hope you are not mad at me. (Pointing
to Bill struggling in the sand)

ANNY

No. Not at all. He deserves to be treated like
that and needs to be punished.

She finds an ugly bucket full of black and grey mud. She sniffs the
disgusting odour, laughs loudly, and splashes it on Bill's desperate-

looking face. She then leaves the latter alone together with the stray dogs.

Their attention is drawn to the sound of music playing in a restaurant not far away.

SUNIL

Can I offer you a drink?

ANNY

With pleasure.

They head for the restaurant.

Soon afterwards, Sunil chats and drinks beers with Anny.

SONG

Later, a Sega dance group arrives on the beach to entertain the public. Sunil and Anny join them for the dance.

ENTER FEW FRIENDS

Some of Bill's friends came looking for him. Bill sees them and starts yelling.

BILL

Hey, I am here. Please help me.

They see him buried in the sand, with only his head poking outside.

They run towards him and starts digging with their hands until they free Bill.

FRIEND ONE

Who did that with you?

Bill looks around. He sees Sunil on the beach far away.

BILL (Enraged, pointing accusatorily)

That bloody rascal sitting over there.

Sunil catches the angry gesture from afar and notices them approaching him. He immediately calls Ram for help.

SCENE 3

INT: GYM

DAY

Ram is lifting weights. He hears his phone ringing. He puts his weights down and goes for the phone.

CUT TO:

PHONE CONVERSATION

SUNIL (V.O)

Hi, iron man. It's your friend Sunil. Remember?

FLASHBACK

Ram is beating those goons in the streets, dispatching them with ease.

SUNIL (V.O)

Ram, come quickly. I am hiding with your girlfriend. The goons are following us. It's time to act!

SUNIL (Talking to himself)

Sorry God, I have to lie!

RAM (Concerned)

Where are you?

SUNIL

On the beach near Restaurant Labourdonnais. Come quickly.

Without hesitation, Ram grabs his bicycle and pedals fiercely towards the location.

MEANWHILE, IN A TENSE HIDEOUT

Sunil and Anny are concealed in a thicket, their breaths heavy with anticipation. Suddenly, they find a group of menacing figures approaching them.

A fight occurs between Sunil and the gang.

Despite Sunil's efforts and his attempt at martial arts, the thugs find his actions amusing rather than threatening.

The gang looks at each other and starts laughing loudly, pointing to Sunil. They find his attempts at combat amusing, bursting into raucous laughter and mockingly pointing at him.

Anny, realizing the gravity of their situation, makes a strategic retreat to the right, hoping to find help or at least draw some attention away from Sunil.

Sunil, now desperate, starts praying, hoping for a miracle or for Ram's timely arrival.

SUNIL

Oh, God, help me.

ONE OF THE GANG MEMBERS (Attempting intimidation)

God won't help.

The mocking laughter is abruptly silenced as they hear a sound behind them. It's Ram, arriving in the nick of time, putting his bicycle down. His presence a clear threat to the gang.

RAM (Confidently)

Of course, he will.

Sunil's fear turns to triumph upon seeing Ram.

SUNIL (Pointing his hands upward, energized)

Yesssss! Hell will descend on you.

Both of them beat the gang members black and blue. While Sunil's fighting style retains a comical edge, they managed to drive the gang away successfully.

Bill and his friends run away.

Ram looks around him, searching for Meera.

RAM

Where is my girlfriend dude?

Sunil, uncertain, looks here and there and points his finger to the wrong direction.

SUNIL

Over there!

Ram searches for his girlfriend but doesn't find her.

SUNIL

Maybe she took off already! Go on, our superhero,
and search for your Barbie girl!

RAM

Please, mate! Let me know when you see her next time. It was not
my luck. I reached late today, but I hope that I can find her soon.

The two friends depart in opposite directions.

Unexpectedly, both Anny and Sunil meet at the bus stop.

SUNIL

Why did you go away?

ANNY

Sorry. I was so frightened.

SUNIL (relieved)

Okay, it's good. No worries.

ANNY

Thank you so much for helping me.

SUNIL (Flirting with Anny)

Do you have the pleasure of accompanying me to a well-known
discotheque where a night party will be held for couples?'

ANNY (Responding positively)

Sure, why not? I will definitely come.

SUNIL

Thrilled you're in. You call me on this number
…! See you at 23:00, princess!

A bus arrives, and she gets on the bus, leaving Sunil waving goodbye.

SUNIL

Bye, baby!

SCENE 4

EXT SHOT: PAMPLEMOUSSES GARDEN

ENTER ZAKA (FELIX'S MAN), MEERA, JOE AND WATCHMAN

Sunil walks towards the garden. His eyes catch the sight of Meera, and a spark ignites within him. He can't help but admire from a distance before making his move.

SUNIL (Talking to himself, with a mix of awe and excitement)

Wow! Such beauty, and here, of all places, alone? What are the odds? Today must be my lucky day

Meera stares at him but then evades Sunil. The moment Meera looks at Sunil, he approaches her and sits on the same bench. He is very enthusiastic to talk to her. Sunil moves closer to Meera.

SUNIL (Smilingly)

Hello…! I'm Sunil!

MEERA (With a polite nod, and a guarded smile)

Hi… I'm Meera!

SUNIL

Hmmm… nice to meet you, Meera!

MEERA

'Well, my pleasure!'

An awkward silence falls between them, filled only by the subtle sounds of the garden. Sunil breaks it, gesturing towards the sky.

SUNIL

Huhhh, nice weather, isn't it?

MEERA

Oh yes, indeed!

Meera is impatient and always looks at the small scarlet flowers on the grass. Sunil notices that. Sunil is also looking at the flowers in the garden. They share a moment of mutual appreciation for the garden's allure.

SUNIL

Such beautiful flowers!

MEERA

Hmm, yeah! They are really eye-catching.

SUNIL (Without hesitating)

May I offer you one? Please! They are only for special people like you.

MEERA

'No, no...! I'm waiting for someone, and
he will come in a few minutes.'

Sunil is disheartened. Far away, he sees a small ice cream seller approaching him.

SUNIL (trying to lighten the mood)

Would you like to have an ice cream?

MEERA (brightening up)

'Yes! Sure!'

Sunil touches his pocket and searches for his wallet or some money. He hesitates.

SUNIL (Embarrassed)

Oh my God, I've forgotten my wallet. I just withdrew Rs 10 000.

MEERA (Dismissively)

Ahh, let it be then! It doesn't matter!

They smile at each other.

MEERA (Half-jokingly)

You have a lot of money, then! Say, could you please transfer Rs10 from your mobile? I've run out of credit.

SUNIL (Eager to impress)

'Of course, dear!

Give me your mobile number, please.'

MEERA (Proudly)

'Ohh, it's …

SUNIL (Instantly)

'Cool! But can I make a request to you if you accept to go to the discotheque at 23:00 tonight? You will receive my phone number soon!'

Sunil transfers Rs10 credit to Meera's phone.

MEERA (Gratefully)

Thanks

Meera saves the number.

MEERA

'Ok, it is fine!'

During their conversation, Sunil tries to seduce her. He goes nearer to
Meera and touches her hand. Sunil is excited.

SUNIL (Excitedly)

'Wait, I'll bring a beautiful flower for you!'

Sunil takes leave. Suddenly, Meera phones someone silently.

Meera (Whispering)

Listen, there's this guy bothering me. Where are you?

As Sunil busies himself with picking the perfect flower, a watchman's
eyes narrow on him, intrigued by his actions.

WATCHMAN

Hey you, what are you doing? It is prohibited to pluck
flowers here! Move your ass, man! Get lost from here!

Sunil is scolded by the watchman. He leaves without saying anything.
He hides near a tree and observes the watchman.

As the watchman continues his patrol, oblivious to Sunil's lingering
presence, a boy casually roams around, and suddenly, an idea passes
his mind. Sunil beckons the boy with a conspirational grin.

SUNIL

Hello, buddy! What's your name?

BOY

Joe!

SUNIL

Nice name! Listen, can you do me a small favor? See that flower bed over there? If you could pluck one flower for me, I'll give you Rs3. You could buy some chocolates with it! What do you say?

JOE (Looking at the flower bed, then Sunil)

Ok!

Joe goes to the garden and quickly plucks some flowers. The watchman spots him. He rapidly comes and shouts at the boy. Sunil is anxious.

SUNIL (Thinking)

I need a flower!

He sees a flower seller with mesmerizing flowers. Sunil approaches the seller.

SUNIL (With genuine admiration)

'Oh! I purchase a flower for the doll.'

Sunil goes to the stall, looking at the flowers with excitement.

SUNIL

Beautiful flowers!

SELLER (Smiling)

Indeed, Sir, they are still fresh from the garden of heaven! Rs5 one flower, Sir! How many would you like? Your girlfriend will be happy and attracted! You could receive several unbelievable kisses with love.

FLASHBACK

Sunil receives a blow from Meera. He moves one meter away from the back.

FLASHBACK ENDS

SUNIL (Astonished)

What! Rs5 for one flower? That's daylight
robbery! <u>They are worth only Rs1.</u>

Sunil, feigning to look for the police, points in a random direction.

SUNIL

I will report you to the police! Look over there!

The seller's attention diverts, searching for the police. Seizing the moment, Sunil quickly grabs a flower, conceals it in his shirt's pocket, and briskly walks away. He returns to Meera and offers the flower.

ZAKA (Felix's gang member) comes in front of them furiously and grips Sunil by his collar.

ZAKA

Who are you? Do you know her? You want to flirt more now?

Sunil is <u>shaken but resists</u>. Zaka then throws him down and takes a knife from his pocket when his mobile phone falls.

ZAKA

Open your mushroom size ears and listen to me
attentively. Next time, be prudent! Stay away from my
girlfriend, or else I'll kill you!' Do you understand?

SUNIL

Yess Sir! Yess Sir!

Both leave Sunil down and move at a really slow pace. Sunil picks Zaka's phone and looks at the screen.

SUNIL (To himself)

Hmmm… photo of that girl! I'll keep it with me
as a souvenir. I said it's a lucky day for me.

Abruptly, he turns the photo, and to his surprise, he reads on the screen

SCREEN

She should be killed before 3 pm!

Sunil is stunned.

Without wasting more time, Sunil shouts at Meera before they go away.

SUNIL (Loudly)

Meera! Be careful… he will kill you!

Zaka looks behind. He sees his phone in Sunil's hand.

Knowing that Sunil is aware of his game, Zaka chases Sunil.

ZAKA (Madly shouting at Sunil)

I will kill you.

The latter hides in a bush.

SUNIL

I will have to take a risk! I will have to face the enemy, so

before anything happens, let me phone the bodybuilder!
It's time to react... Sorry God... I have to lie again!

He removes his phone and talks to Ram while running.

SUNIL

Hey dude, I've found your girl. Where are you?

SCENE 5

INT SHOT: RAM'S ROOM

Ram practises martial arts in his room. He moves through fluid, precise forms of martial arts with a quiet intensity.

RAM

What?

The focus shifts from his disciplined solitude to urgency. He listens to Sunil, then with quick, decisive actions, he throws on a shirt, snatches his bike helmet, and goes to Pamplemousses Garden.

SUNIL

Sorry, God. I have to lie. I don't even know who Ram's girlfriend is! But I've got to do something, now's the time.

SCENE 6

EXT SHOT: PAMPLEMOUSSES GARDEN

ENTER: SUNIL, MEERA, ZAKA, POLICE AND RAM

The serene beauty of Pamplemousses Garden is shattered by the sound of hurried footsteps. Sunil swiftly hides behind a thick bush. Meera, her face a mask of terror and determination, tries to follow, desperate to understand the unfolding situation.

ZAKA (tauntingly)

You think you are smart? Today is your last day on earth!

He starts beating him.

Sunil tries to shield himself, when suddenly…

RAM

Leave him alone.

Ram steps into the fray with a determined look on his face.

SUNIL (Relief washing over)

Ram is here! Oh, my hero! You are not just iron
man, but you're also The Fall Guy.

With a flurry of movement, Ram engages in the skirmish, quickly turning the tide. Zaka, overwhelmed and injured, collapses onto the grass. The sound of police sirens fills the air, prompting Zaka to scramble to his feet and flee.

A police jeep comes full of police officers.

SUNIL (Panting, calling the POLICE OFFICER)

Officer, officer… save me! He wants to kill me.

POLICE OFFICER (Skeptical)

What? Maybe you did something wrong, and that's why he is running after you. Where is he?

RAM (Stepping in)

I am an eyewitness to what happened, sir. They were trying to beat him. But they ran away when they heard the police siren. This man here is a victim.

POLICE OFFICER (Nodding, still cautious)

Ok. Be careful.

The police officers scan the surroundings, but they see no one. They let Sunil go.

RAM (Anxious)

Where is my girlfriend?

SUNIL

Oh no, I think she's gone again! I think she is not too far. She must be around.

Ram goes in search of Meera. The urgency in their actions contrasts sharply with the tranquil backdrop of Pamplemousses Garden, leaving the scene charged with a mix of adrenaline and concern.

ENTER MEERA AND SUNIL

SAME GARDEN

Sunil laughs loudly.

SUNIL (Playfully)

Hey dear, I have this friend I pretend doesn't exist whenever I find myself in a tight spot. Every time I meet a girl, I claim she's the apple of his eye. Works like a charm; he can't resist showing up!

MEERA (Reproachfully)

That is unfair, Sunil.

SUNIL (Dismissively)

Forget about all that. Let's just enjoy ourselves. How about a dance?

Sunil draws out his mobile phone and puts on an upbeat track. They sway, and move around doing a lively dance.

THE DANCE ENDS

SUNIL (Admiringly)

You're a good dancer, dear! Are you sure you will accompany me to the disco tonight?

MEERA

Sure, why not!

SUNIL

See you gorgeous at 23:00 tonight at Volume Club!

Sunil laughs mockingly. Everyone departs.

Ram is riding his bicycle and sees Meera.

RAM

Oh, that's my girlfriend! That guy was not wrong!

While Zaka was hiding, he flinches when he receives a phone call.

FELIX

Did you find her? Where is she

ZAKA (Nervously)

Yes, boss! She slipped away. Your contract is scheduled
for 3 o'clock, and I'm making my move!

FELIX

You fool, be quick on your mission! I want her dead asap!
She is a big threat to us, you fool. Go and get her now!

EXT SHOT

LOCATION: IN THE STREET

ENTER: ZAKA, RAJ, GANG AND MEERA

ZAKA (Determined, the figure of Meera approaching his sights)

Don't worry, boss. Your work will be done; she is in front of me!

Zaka blocks Meera.

ZAKA (Menacingly)

So, here you are. Who's going to save you now?

Once again, a voice disrupts him from behind.

RAM

She doesn't need saving. But you might. Back off

Zaka turns his head and exclaims.

ZAKA (Frustrated)

Oh no. It's you again. Leave us alone. This is none of your business.

RAM (Adamantly)

As long as you keep bothering her, this will always be my business.

A fight happens between Ram and the gang, including Zaka. Ram punches those men so hard that Zaka falls heavily to the ground. His men can't fight against Ram as he is too strong for them.

In the chaos, Meera seizes her chance and runs away…

SCENE 7

EXT SHOT: SEASIDE

ENTER: SUNIL, RAJ, TOURIST & POLICE

Sunil is strolling along the seaside. He is looking at RAJ (a thief), wearing sunglasses, walking by, and searching for money from purses and wallets he has robbed. Raj checks the first wallet, finds nothing and throws it away. He checks the second purse.

RAJ (Muttering to himself)

It seems that the poor Raj will not get anything either.

He throws it.

He again looks around and takes out a third wallet from his pocket.

RAJ

There is no money in this wallet also. Bad luck man

But he finds one rupee. He wants to throw the purse but did not do that. He had a second thought.

RAJ

This one is new and beautiful. I will keep it.

He looks at the wallet cautiously.

RAJ

I could sell it.

He puts it back in his pocket. He speedily searches for money in the next few wallets left. He takes cash from each wallet and then throws the wallets one by one when he suddenly notices an ugly old wallet. He laughs out loudly.

RAJ

Can I get something from you, old wallet?

He opens the wallet, and to his great surprise, he finds a winning horse receipt.

RAJ

Noble Wages Rs200 for Rs4000! I won!.Hooray!

He raises his hands in excitement, but unfortunately, the receipt slips from his hand and goes right into the water.

RAJ

Oh, no, no, no! Not like this!

He frantically tries to retrieve it with a stick, but it was so wet that it got torn.

RAJ (Staring at the torn ticket)

Just my luck.

Raj phones a friend to lament his misfortune

RAJ

Hello, my receipt is useless now. It dropped it into
the water, and it's torn and wet as well.

FRIEND (over the phone)

It's a waste of time to place a bet at a bookmaker who gives
receipts. But it is safe to place bets with a bookmaker,
who will deposit the winning ticket money into your
account, and thus, there will be no receipt, and no tension.
Your money will be safe. Next time, be careful!'

Sunil takes the fishing rod and goes fishing. He wears a homemade
sign: "1 lb fish for Rs25" around his neck and waits for a client. He
begins to hum a tune.

Raj passes by, and notices the board that Sunil hung around his neck.

RAJ

What? one pound of fish for only Rs25? I
will have a good fish curry today.

Raj <u>hastily</u> takes a Rs100 note.

RAJ

Here is Rs100. Give me two kilos of fish and keep the change.

Sunil looks at Raj greedily.

SUNIL (Enthusiastically)

'Have patience; I will fish fresh fish directly
from the sea. Just for you, my friend!'

RAJ (Skeptical)

You don't have any fish with you.

SUNIL

No, my friend. I only sell freshly caught fish. My clients
love that. They know what they are eating.

RAJ (nodding, convinced)

OK. It sounds good. I will be waiting for you.

Sunil takes the fishing rod, puts the bait in it, and throws it in the sea.
Raj is patiently waiting.

RAJ (To himself)

I'll have a good dinner with my family tonight.

SUNIL (Cunningly)

The bait is not good. The fish is not eating it. Look, I have
kept my belongings here. Keep an eye on them. I will fetch my
professional equipment and share my catch with you. A big fish.

RAJ

OK. But hurry up. I am craving for a good curry fish.

Sunil leaves the fishing rod with Raj.

SUNIL

Be back in a jiffy!

RAJ

I, myself, could do the fishing job. Let me enjoy my free time.

Raj throws the fishing line into the sea, but he is unaware that his
fishing line goes to his back and gets hooked in a tourist's shirt sitting
by the side of the sea, busy enjoying the sun. The tourist approaches Raj.

TOURIST (Irritated)

Eh… Stupid! You have caught my shirt with your hook!
I am taking a rest, and you are disturbing me.

RAJ (Angrily)

Is this a place to rest here? Go home and rest in your bed.

TOURIST (Fuming, cussing in French)

In France, it is not like this.

RAJ

But this is not France, my friend. Go and take your sunbath further.

The tourist takes leave, exasperated.

Raj remembers Sunil's belongings (in fact, they were those of the tourist), kicks them two times, takes them, and walks away. The tourist sees Raj going away with his belongings, and starts shouting.

TOURIST

Thief! Thief!

Raj flees away. Some patrolling policemen go in his pursuit, and they catch Raj.

POLICEMAN

We were looking for someone who was stealing tourists' belongings. So that's you. We caught your hand in the bag.

RAJ (Desperately)

No, no! I am not a robber. These are my friend's belongings.
I was on my way to give them back to him.

At the exact moment, Sunil passes by and looks at Raj.

RAJ

Look, look! That's him. Hello, my friend.

SUNIL

I don't know that man. Put him behind bars.
These thieves are such a nuisance.'

SCENE 7

EXT SHOT: SEASIDE

ENTER: SUNIL, FELIX, YOUSUF, ANDREW, SEVDOU, LILY AND RAM

Sunil laughs and goes away with a bottle of juice in his hand. He finds a millionaire, FELIX, in his brand-new luxurious car with his young wife, LILY.

SUNIL (Staring at the lady)

One day I will get a reward and of course,
girls like this... God will gift me.

Sunil starts observing Lily walking on the beach.

SUNIL (Talking to himself, looking at the young lady in her bikini)

Wow, what a sexy girl! She is not only cool
but very hot in her sexy bikini also.

SUNIL (Talking to himself)

I need to go out with her!

His gaze then shifts back to Felix, who has by now joined Lily in the gentle waves. Both laughing and enjoying the water. Sunil imagines he is swimming with her.

Sunil has a short glimpse.

SUNIL (Talking to himself)

Hey fatso, you don't know me yet. Wait, I'll show you who I am..

Sunil looks at Felix's clothes and car, a Mercedes Benz…

SUNIL (Talking to himself)

He must be a rich fellow. Watch, I make you poor.

Sunil takes Lily' clothes and examines them one by one. He even sniffs her sexy skirt and smiles.

SUNIL

Good perfume!

He keeps it at the place quietly and laughs. He looks at the millionaire's clothes furiously and runs away with them.

SUNIL

These ugly clothes!

He arrives near the region where the water is deepest and looks at Felix, who is still swimming. He looks at his clothes and becomes tense.

SUNIL (Talking to himself)

He is pretending to be smart and young.

He throws all of Felix's clothes in the water. He laughs and goes away. Unexpectedly, he stops and holds his head.

SUNIL (Talking to himself)

I'm really an idiot. Instead of throwing the clothes, I should have worn them. But it doesn't matter next time.

Sunil finds some beautiful beachwear clothes lying under a filao tree. He looks everywhere and sees nobody. He starts wearing them. The phone rings, and he looks at the phone. His sister's name, SEVDOU, appears. Sunil switches off the phone.

SUNIL (Talking to himself)

Stop annoying me, sister.

He switches off the phone call

He wears a CHAPEAU LAPAILLE and avocado shorts and a shirt with a hibiscus flower design. He looks at himself and laughs. Sunil is still walking and ANDREW looking at his clothes.

SUNIL

Hey, mister, is it the first time you have seen such beautiful clothes?

ANDREW

I'm really sorry, but your clothes are really attractive!

SUNIL (Laughing)

I know that. Tell me something new I don't know about me.'

Sunil moves, looking again and again at the back. He sits in an old wooden varnish chair and observes

Felix is going toward his belongings and sees that his clothes are missing.

FELIX (Screaming)

Where are my clothes?!!

YOUSEF and Andrew hear the screaming and come running.

YOUSEF

What happened, boss?

FELIX

My clothes are missing. Someone tricked me. You must find him.

Andrew remembers Sunil's clothes.

ANDREW

It must be the guy I saw. He was wearing clothes that were
too expensive for him. He has worn our clothes too.

FELIX

So, what are you waiting for? Go and get him. My honour is at stake.

Yousuf and Andrew take their motorbike with their mobile phone in
their hands and are about to go in search of Sunil.

ANDREW

Wherever he is, we will find him.

Sunil has been observing the scene from far away. He knows he won't
escape easily. He starts running.

SUNIL

Oh! This is a bad omen. I am in danger!

Sunil takes out his phone and calls Ram.

SUNIL

Hey! Dude! Your girlfriend is at the beach. She looks
very sexy, but goons follow her. Come quickly, man!

RAM (VOICE ON PHONE)

Keep an eye on her, dude. I am on my way.

SCENE 8

EXT SHOT

LOCATION: IN THE STREET

ENTER: SUNIL, ANDREW, YOUSEF, RAHUL, YOUSEF'S WIFE

Sunil is very vigilant. He hears a motorbike coming and hides himself. After the motorcycle is gone, he laughs.

While walking, he notices again another motorbike coming. He looks for another place to hide but can't find anything. Sunil sees a box. He wraps himself <u>into</u> the box and starts walking.

He hears the two guys talking.

ANDREW

> Yousef, have you noticed anything?

YOUSEF

Nothing, Andrew.

ANDREW

Boss will be furious if we don't find him. My honour is at stake (imitating Felix's voice). Let's continue looking.

Sunil comes to learn that they are Andrew and Yousef. He stops walking immediately.

YOUSEF

Why did the box stop walking?

ANDREW

'Yeah… now it is not walking.'

The box starts moving, and Sunil falls down.

SUNIL (Screams in pain)

Owwww!

Both Andrew and Yousef are now frightened.

ANDREW (Panicking)

It is evil. Run!.

YOUSEF (Muttering, frightened)

Gh-gho… Ghost!

ANDREW

Ghost!

They get on their motorcycles and drive away quickly but knock against a wall and fall into the muddy water. Sunil opens the box, laughs, and goes away.

SUNIL (Talking to himself)

I have learned these acting skills for a long time.

Andrew and Yousef are searching for him with sticks in their hands. They are riding a motorbike and are looking for Sunil. Yousef's phone rings. His wife is calling him.

YOUSEF'S WIFE

'Hello, where are you wandering?'

YOUSEF

I am working, darling.

YOUSEF'S WIFE

Are you working, or are you with another
woman? When will you be home?

YOUSEF

You know that you are the only woman in
my life. I will be home in one hour.

YOUSEF'S WIFE

You better be on time. If not, you know what will happen to you.

Yousef jumps like spring, and the phone falls down.

They stop to pick up the mobile phone.

Andrew and Yousuf see some clothes dangling on a rope in a yard.

ANDREW

Hey Yousef, look at these clothes. I bet they
will fit me. Let's go and get them.

Andrew climbs the gate, which is closed.

Andrew is taking the outfits when someone sees him. Andrew is wearing the clothes. RAHUL approaches with a pistol, and when Andrew tries to climb the gate, he points the gun on his shoulder from the back.

RAHUL

Remove the clothes from your body. If you
don't do it, I shall shoot you.

From the back, Andrew is removing the clothes when the man, Rahul, notices him.

RAHUL

Andrew, it's you? What has happened to you? Without clothes!

ANDREW

Excuse me. A thief has stolen all my clothes.

ANDREW

I know well how my wife is, and she will
kill me if I go home like this.

RAHUL

No problem, you can wear these clothes, my friend
but on one condition; wear my wife's sexy sleeveless
shirt; otherwise, I will shoot at you!'

ANDREW (In disbelief)

What?! Are you kidding?

RAHUL (Threateningly)

No. I am all serious. Execute, or I shoot.

Andrew wears the clothes rapidly without realising they are very loose.

RAHUL

As quickly as possible, put one on my wife's shoes lying
in the bin! You fool, take only one of them.

Andrew wears the right high heels shoes, while his left leg is bare-footed.
He advances stumblingly and falls down. He gets up, looks here and
there, and is about to leave.

Rahul opens the gate, and Andrew runs rapidly towards the motorbike
where Yousef, in tiny shorts and a vest, is waiting for him.

YOUSEF

What happened? You are wearing a ladies' dress.

ANDREW

Hurry! Let's get out from here; otherwise,
we will be 6 feet under the earth.

On his way, Andrew's pants fall off. He pulls it up and climbs the motorbike.

Rahul fires in the air, and they flee away. While running away, they almost hit Ram with the bike.

ANDREW

You!!!!!!! Ugly rotten egg!!!!! Move away!

They pull Ram's shirt.

Ram follows them while they run away.

SCENE 9

AFTERNOON SHOOT

FADE IN

INT: STREET

ENTER: TWO LADIES, JAMES, MEERA, RAM, DRIVER AND SUNIL

Sunil stands on the pavement, holding a black lady's plastic bag in his hand.

SUNIL

The bag will be enough as I must go a long way.

He is trying to stop some cars. He waves his hand as he sees cars coming.

SUNIL

Lift, please!

DRIVER (Angrily)

Get out of the way, you idiot. You want to be killed.

Sunil looks at the cars desolately. He moves by the roadside to stop cars. He sees another car coming in his direction. Rapidly, he tries to move on the road.

He waves his hand again as the car comes closer. He tries to move towards the car.

SUNIL (To himself)

Hey! Dear, I am not foolish. I realized that the car was not going to stop because it was moving very fast and that the car might hit me.

Quickly, he moves towards the pavement and falls down.

SUNIL (To himself)

Hey you… Driving fast means dying fast. One should not drive so fast, or else he will find himself in a cemetery. Be careful.

He rises up, picks up his bag, and puts it on his shoulder. He then looks on the ground and scratches his head as he nods.

SUNIL (Talking to himself)

Now, I must definitely get a car! I can't wait here anymore.

He decides to stop a car in the middle of the road. He moves his two hands widely to stop another car that will come.

Suddenly, he gets an idea. He rushes to the corner to pick up a big stone. He puts it on the right side and lies on the left side of the road.

SUNIL (Talking to himself)

One car shall obviously stop now.

He waits, but no car is coming. He is very disappointed. Finally, he sees a car coming from very far away.

SUNIL

It's a taxi.

Quickly, Sunil removes the stone. He rushes to the middle of the road and opens his two arms widely while shouting to stop. The taxi is now forced to stop. The driver peeps from the window.

DRIVER

Do you want to die? Get off the road, or else I'll drive on you.

SUNIL

Do you want to go to jail or help me? Sir, sir, someone
has stolen my bicycle. I don't know how to get home.
Could you please give me a lift to my house?

DRIVER (Sighing)

Okay, okay. Where are you going?

SUNIL

At Vallee des Pretres. It's not far away.

DRIVER

Okay. Get inside.

The driver accepts, and Sunil gets into the car. Meera is in the car, reading a book. She ignores Sunil. Sunil's phone rings. It is Ram.

RAM (Calling on the phone)

I can't find my girl.

Sunil is looking at Meera. He smiles at her.

SUNIL

She might have gone, dear!

RAM

Don't forget my words!

SUNIL

Sure, bro!

The driver hits the brakes and stops the car.

DRIVER

Rs100 for the lift.

SUNIL

What? I have to pay for a lift. I have no money with me.

The driver glances at him.

DRIVER

By the way, what's in your bag?

SUNIL

There are some fishes in it.

The driver looks at the big bag in an enchanted way as he rubs both of his palms.

DRIVER

Give them to me.

Sunil hurriedly holds his bag tightly.

SUNIL

These are for my mother, and if I don't bring them home today,
I won't have the right to step into the house, but if you agree,
we can go together to cook them and have it together.

The driver quickly and secretly turns off the engine.

DRIVER

Oh my God!

Sunil turns towards the driver.

SUNIL

What happened?

DRIVER

The car broke down. We must push the car so it can start again.

Sunil looks at the driver suspiciously

DRIVER

Go out and push the car quickly!

Sunil takes his bag and tries to alight from the taxi.

DRIVER

The bag will get in the way you when you
push the car. Leave it inside, my boy.

SUNIL (Reluctantly)

Okay. Keep it safe.

DRIVER

No worries, my boy. It's in safe hands.

Sunil puts the bag on the seat and gets out from the car. The driver looks at the bag pleasantly and rubs both palms again. He throws a twenty-rupee coin out the window, turns on the engine, and drives away quickly. Sunil runs after the car.

SUNIL (Shouting, attempting to chase the car)

Hey you, stop the car and give me my bag full of fish.

Sunil laughs in humiliation as he picks up the coin.

SUNIL

He was very easy to fool.

Sunil notices Ram and says hello by sign.

RAM

Hey! Mate, don't forget to call me when you see my girlfriend!

SUNIL

'Yes, dear!'

A car halts, and Ram rides unnoticed.

DRIVER

One should rob a man like this as he seems to be a fool.

He takes his mobile and dials his wife's mobile number.

DRIVER

Hello, darling… Buy a bottle of wine quickly, my doll,
because I'm bringing something special to eat.

The driver takes the bag and looks inside it. The car stops. He finds banana peel in the bag. He throws the bag out of the window.

DRIVER (Disgustingly)

Ah, shit!

JAMES is walking promptly and slips on the banana peel. On seeing James, Sunil drops the coin. James comes and picks it up.

SUNIL

Hey, you fellow! It's mine!

James watches him and the coin several times.

JAMES

Oh, take it! I'm sorry!

Sunil notices two beautiful ladies coming in his direction. He drops the money discreetly. They are astounded to see the Rs20 coin in front of them. Both of them grab the money.

BOTH OF THEM (Fighting)

It's mine! It's mine!

Sunil arrives as a blind person and touches the ladies' hands.

SUNIL

Oh, my friend! Did you find a Rs20 coin? I just lost it.

LADY (1)

Yes. Sure!

They look at Sunil in puzzlement. He touches their hands sensationally several times. They look at him in sadness, and give him the coin and leave.

THE LADIES (SAME TIME)

·Poor man

FADE TO BLACK

SCENE 10

EXT SHOT: BEACH

ENTER: SUNIL, MAN, AND BEGGAR

Sunil sits on a bench along a bustling beachside street. A well and typically dressed man is sitting next to him. He keeps the coin on the bench. The MAN soon notices the coin. He picks it up. Sunil stops him. Sunil tries to signal a policeman who is patrolling.

SUNIL

Excuse me, but I believe that you have just taken my Rs20 coin?

MAN

Sorry! Sorry! Sir.

SUNIL

Do you want me to call that policeman?

MAN (Anxious)

No, please, don't do that! Here!!!!! Take this Rs200!!!!

He hands Sunil a Rs200 note and walks away.

Sunil gives the BEGGARRs100.

SUNIL

Take this, my friend. You must be starving.

BEGGAR (Overwhelmed)

Thank you, Sir. God will bless you and your family.

SCENE 11

LOCATION: SMS PARIAZ BOOKMAKER

ENTER: SUNIL

Sunil enters SMS PARIAZ BOOKMAKER, places a bet and comes back. Outside he checks his mobile for updates

SUNIL (Relieved)

Oh! My horse won. Now, I place a bet on 3-4.

SCENE 12

LOCATION: GREEN DRAGON RESTAURANT AT QUATRE BORNES

ENTER: DON & JOHN (FELIX ENEMY), SUNIL AND A LADY

Sunil reaches the Green Dragon Restaurant. He enjoys the 3rd race coming on the TV.

SUNIL (Elated)

Oh! My horse number 4 won. I can taste a better meal. Waiter!

WAITER

Yes Sir. What can I do for you?

SUNIL

Give me your best special fried noodles and a cold Coke.

Sunil notices Felix

Sunil approaches him in a very friendly way. Felix is heavily drunk.

SUNIL

Are you fine?

FELIX (In a friendly way, slurring)

I'm alright! Just finished a bottle of Black Label. I'm Felix and you?

SUNIL

I'm Sunil, the innocent man.

They shake hands. Felix laughs.

FELIX (Laughing)

I can see you as a man, Sunil!

Felix is looking at Sunil from head to toe.

FELIX (Teasingly)

Are you a boy or a girl?

SUNIL (Amused)

You can take me as whom you want. That don't matter.

FELIX (Laughing)

I really like your manner. Would you like to have something?

SUNIL

Yes, with pleasure. Same as you.

Sunil is eating and chatting with <u>him</u>. Felix pays the bill, and they leave.

SCENE 13

LOCATION: IN THE STREETS

ENTER: FELIX, DON, JOHN, SUNIL AND LILY

Felix and Sunil are walking along the street.

SUNIL (Glancing around warily)

Be careful of moving cars!

But no vehicles can be seen! The street is eerily devoid of any such danger.

FELIX

It seems I hear something.

SUNIL

Please be <u>cautious,</u> as an elephant can walk on you here.

Felix holds Sunil tightly. Sunil looks badly at him and pushes him. As he is heavily drunk, he misses a few steps and slips and knocks against a tree. He is <u>startled</u>.

SUNIL

Light up a cigarette down the tree, or anything can happen to you.

FELIX (Skeptically)

No, I don't believe in all these things... protector

SUNIL

Oh, you must. I had a friend of mine. He was drunk and sat
under a tree swearing. When he got home, he saw a long, skinny
man in his dream. He was calling him by his name. He said that
he disrespected him for the tree belonged to him. Afterwards,
my friend fell ill and died a week later. So, I advise you to
light a cigarette and not to offend any soul under the tree.

FELIX (Clearly afraid)

Now you're scaring me.

Felix hesitantly lights a cigarette.

As the two proceed, DON and JOHN, catch up, accidentally collides
with Sunil in the process.

DON (Apologetically)

Sorry.

His cellular phone falls down.

Sunil secretly picks Don's phone, <u>switches it off,</u> puts it in his pocket,
and catches up with Felix.

They walk in the direction of Felix's house. When they reach his house,
Felix opens his gate.

SUNIL

<u>Shall I come in?</u>

FELIX

Yeah, of course! <u>But</u> my wife is not here!

SUNIL (Suddenly changing his mind, backing)

Umm, no, I can't. I should actually head home. It's getting late. My mum is waiting for me to drink soup, eat roasted chicken, eat ice cream and... Ok, next time!

SUNIL (Talking to himself)

Hmmm, where has that beautiful lady gone?
Oh, but when will she return?

SUNIL (To Felix)

By the way, what's her name?

FELIX

Who?

SUNIL

Your wife?

FELIX

Oops... Lily!

SUNIL (Thinking)

Hmmm, just like the lily flower...wow...
Lily darling. Just come into my arms!

Sunil gets lost in a daydream. He imagines himself dancing with Lily very romantically.

(clips)

Felix watches him as he moves, utterly baffled, eyes wide open, and holding his bottle.

FELIX (Amused)

What are you doing?

SUNIL (Still daydreaming)

Be careful… Lily!

When Felix hears his wife's name, Lily, he drops his bottle. Sunil, caught off guard, misses a step and falls down, but recovers quickly, returning to reality.

FELIX (Angrily)

You rascal! You are here for my wife. Get away from here!

Sunil tries to escape while he robs Felix's wallet.

FELIX (Outraged)

Hey! Give me my wallet, you bastard. You don't know who I am?

SUNIL (Tauntingly, as he makes his escape)

Just a drunken dude who is about to lose his wallet and his wife.

Sunil kicks Felix's buttock, gets out, and checks both the phone and wallet.

SUNIL (Talking to himself)

Well done, Sunil… You've killed two birds with one stone.

SCENE 14

EXT: IN THE STREET

ENTER: YOUSEF, SUNIL, ANDREW AND VITAL

Andrew is riding a motorbike with his friend Yousuf. They notice Sunil. Their mobile phones ring, and they panic. Their wives are on the line.

YOUSEF'S WIFE (On the phone)

Where are you? You told me you will be home
in one hour. I am coming to find you.

YOUSEF

Yes, my baby, I'm at the Shop X. Okay, okay, you can come.'

Yousef hangs up the phone.

Andrew, in the meantime, is also on the phone with his wife.

ANDREW

Hello, my doll. I'm on my way, just coming home. Umm… I'm
near the Ajageer Saree Palace. What? You are coming here!

Andrew hangs up while adjusting his pants...

ANDREW

Oh shit… my wife is coming here.

YOUSEF

'My wife too!' What will we do now?

ANDREW

Let's find that scoundrel first. If not, the boss is gonna freak out.

CUT TO:

Sunil, panic-stricken, darts into a dimly lit alley and ducks under a veranda, seeking refuge in the shadows. The darkness is oppressive, but fear propels him forward. He bumps into a shadowy figure, Vital, a man whose presence commands attention.

SUNIL (Desperately)

Help me, please. Some bad guys are after me.

VITAL (Narrowing his eyes)

Why? Have you robbed them?

SUNIL

No, no. They are trying to rob me.

VITAL

Bloody robbers, Hein. Come. I'll hide you.

As Sunil attempts to follow, he hesitates, scanning the dark for more threats. Suddenly, Vital makes out Sunil's silhouette. In a moment of panic, Vital, mistaking Sunil for an intruder, swings an old, rusted pan, striking Sunil on the head.

Before the situation escalates further Yousef and Andrew make their appearance. Vital confronts them with a fierce bravado.

VITAL

Go away otherwise…

ANDREW (Smirking)

Otherwise, what? You think we will get scared with this rotten pan?

VITAL (Defiantly)

Huh! Yes!!

Vital shows them the old rotten pan

Vital manages to push Andrew, causing him to stumble. His loose pants begin to slip. Embarrassed, Andrew quickly grabs it with both hands. Andrew and Yousef retreat.

VITAL

This is my property, and nobody is allowed to come in.

Suddenly, Sunil regains consciousness. They are looking at each other.

SUNIL

Vital… it's you. How are you, my friend?

VITAL

Don't ask me about that. Do you remember at the hospital? Dr. Fousad did so many injections with me that now there are large holes everywhere in my body, especially on my buttocks. Wait, I'll show you.

<u>Vital undressing</u>

<u>SUNIL</u>

<u>No, don't show me. I believe you, my friend.</u>

Suddenly, Sunil notices Yousef and Andrew from a distance.

SUNIL

Beware, my friend. They are still here looking for us.

He hides behind some big plastic bins. Vital has no idea what Sunil wants to do with his shocking actions.

VITAL

What are you trying to do with this bin?

SUNIL

Vital, come! Cover me! Quick… Quick… Quickly!

There is waste inside <u>the box, and it</u> falls on Sunil. He then tries to walk with the bin. He slips on a plastic bottle and tumbles to the ground.

VITAL (Chuckling)

This guy is as mad as me. But what a good idea.

SUNIL

Aaaaahhhhh…!

VITAL

Are you okay, man?

SUNIL

Ya, ya… push me, push me, and let's go!

Vital starts pushing the bin with Sunil inside. Sunil screams and rolls toward Yousef and Andrew.

Hearing the screams and noises, they realise that as the street is steep, the bin will head towards them

They run away. While running, Andrew struggles with his slipping pant, clumsily running with a woman's shoe on one foot.

Sunil is relieved.

Abruptly, he sees them again near the restaurant. Swiftly, he hides himself and observes them. Sunil notices a woman holding a plastic bag of flour and going. He runs to her, snatches the flour, and throws it on their faces.

SUNIL

Take this, you, scoundrel!

ANDREW

You moron, what have you done?

YOUSEF

I can't see anything!

They are standing on the entrance mat of the restaurant. Sunil, without wasting time, grabs that carpet from their feet, pulls it, watching them as they crash to the ground. Sunil finds an electric cable hanging from a nearby pole. A mischievous idea strikes him.

SUNIL

Be prepared to get roasted like peanuts.

With a swift movement, he pulls it and places the wire on them.

ANDREW AND YOUSUF (Screaming together)

NO, NO, NO!

They jump to their feet, narrowly avoiding the sparks. Their ordeal ends with them feeling in a comic, haphazard sprint

SCENE 15

LOCATION: THE GREEN DRAGON RESTAURANT

ENTER: SUNIL, VITAL, BOUNCER, MEERA

Sunil brings Vital to the same restaurant. Two bouncers are standing at the restaurant door. They welcome Sunil and Vital.

SUNIL

Don't you know that you should say Good Afternoon, sir!?

The two bouncers feel hesitated and greeted them.

BOUNCERS

Good afternoon, sir!

Bon après-midi monsieur!

SUNIL (Arrogantly)

That's it! It's okay!

They take a seat. Vital looks at Sunil hesitantly.

VITAL

Wow! Look at that place. It must be very expensive here?

SUNIL (Smiling sarcastically)

Vital, don't worry! I will pay the bill. So, chill out and enjoy!

VITAL

Really, mate?

SUNIL (With full attitude and arrogance)

'Hey, waiter, ask your people to put some
music, please, or else I'll do it myself.'

(CLIPS)

Sunil picks up his spoon and fork and starts making sounds with the glass. Even Vital joins him by tapping the plates. They are dancing and making noises in the restaurant. Everyone is watching them.

Waiters bring all kinds of food, both of them eat voraciously.

VITAL (With food in his mouth)

It's so delicious. Thank you, my friend.

SUNIL (Mouth full of food)

You're welcome. Just enjoy.

Sunil is analysing the atmosphere of the place when he sees the gorgeous Meera having dinner with her parents.

SUNIL

Oh, the princess is here! Her presence is a bad omen for
me. Hope this time nothing wrong will happen!

SUNIL

I have a vision flashing in my mind. I have a déjà vu,

and some goons are after me inside the restaurant,
so I have to call Ram again for protection.

He wakes up. Moves here and there

SUNIL

No, no, no,! This can't happen! I better get hold of myself
and think positively. Pouff! Let me have some kebab and
beer. It will help me relax a bit. Yes, let me do that.

CONTINUES....

LOCATION: GREEN DRAGON RESTAURANT AT QUATRE
BORNES

ENTER: TOMMY AND A GOON, A CHILD, TINY AND A LADY,
ANNICK, SUNIL, MEERA

SUNIL

Now, surely there will be some problems!'

TOMMY looks here and there, gets up, and moves towards the
washroom. Sunil finds it fishy. Something is wrong.

SUNIL

I find Tommy's behaviour weird, as if he is hiding something.

So, Sunil curiously goes to listen to his conversation. Tommy goes inside
the washroom to call someone.

Sunil is lost in his thoughts when he hears Tommy talking to Felix
over the phone.

TOMMY (Talking to Felix)

Felix, why were you not picking up the phone? The

photographer in the red dress (Meera) and the young guy with the bicycle have been found. Both will also be killed soon!'

SUNIL

Now, I have no choice. I have to call Ram straight away and inform him that his life and that of Meera are in danger.

Sunil peeps from the window.

SUNIL (Thinking)

Oh gosh!!!!! It's the iron man, always with his bicycle! I should call him.

Sunil, without wasting time, calls Ram.

RAM

Hello, dude. Have you seen my girlfriend?

SUNIL (His voice sounds stressed)

Hey dude, listen carefully. Some goons are after your life! They are the same goons with whom you fought while protecting the girl…remember, your fight in the streets?

RAM

The same ones.

SUNIL

Yes, the same goons! They are here, in front of me.

RAM

But where are you?

SUNIL

At the Green Dragon restaurant in Quatre Bornes. I
just overheard their conversation about killing you and
a girl. Where are you? Come here immediately. Sorry
mate, this time, your charming princess is not here!'

RAM

Don't worry, my friend, I will be there in a minute.

SUNIL (Talking to himself)

Thank God, I am not a liar now!

SCENE 16

LOCATION: INSIDE RAM'S ROOM

Ram takes his bicycle and gun from his drawer and leaves home.

RAM

I will teach those goons a big lesson this time.

CONTINUES....

ENTER: SUNIL, VITAL, WAITER, BOUNCERS

SUNIL (Talking to himself)

But who might be the girl in the red dress? Well, never mind!

Sunil is running from the back door, looking at Vital repeatedly.

SUNIL

'Vital has eaten well; now see the outcome!'

Vital is looking here and there with confusion. Two bouncers are worried. Vital bows his head. Waiters, come and take the plates away and then the spoons. One waiter brings the bill and then looks at Vital again and again.

WAITER (1)

Will he be able to pay the bill or not? Let us go and ask.

VITAL (Confused & Scared)

My friend was about to pay the bill, but I don't
know where he has suddenly vanished.

WAITER (1)

If he is gone, you have to pay the bill yourself,
or you will be in big trouble.

Two bouncers come.

BOUNCER (1)

What happened? Hurry up! You have to pay the bill right now!

VITAL (Terrified)

I don't even have a single penny with me, so how will I pay the bill?

The bouncers start beating Vital.

VITAL (In pain)

I explain to you what has happened.

He talks in sign and succeeds in getting their attention.

VITAL

Stop, stop, please? A guy called Sunil brought me
here. He said he would pay the bills. I swear.

BOUNCER

Where is he now?

VITAL

I don't know. He went to the toilet, and I haven't seen him since.

The bouncers stop beating Vital. They start listening to him. The manager of the restaurant arrives and comes to know about the whole situation.

MANAGER

What is happening? This is too much noise.
It's not good for the clients.

BOUNCER

This man says he is not able to pay the bills. A man named Sunil brought him here and told him he would pay. But he since vanished.

MANAGER

Here is my card, and whenever you see your friend, just give me a call. I will teach him a lesson, but you must pay for the food you have eaten! You should work in my restaurant!

While carrying out his tasks, he pays attention to something and smiles broadly.

VITAL

Sir, I am going to clean over there!

MANAGER

Okay, and make it fast! There is a lot of
pending work! Come on, hurry up!

CONTINUES....

ENTER: VITAL, ANNICK, FAMILY, TOMMY AND THE GANG, AND TINY

Vital walks towards a table occupied by a family of four persons having dinner (ANNICK, TINY, TOMMY and the GANG). He drops his cleaning cloth just behind the lady while walking. As he lifts it up, he ties the lady, Annick's ribbon dress, to the chair. Vital quickly withdraws himself and observes them. She realises that something is wrong with her dress. Right at that moment, Vital drops water on her son's pants. She looks dreadfully at her son.

ANNICK

You have spoiled your pants, you crazy kid! Tiny, grow up!

Annick is furious. Tiny is confused, unaware of what he has done wrong.

TINY

What? What have I done? Why are you saying that?

ANNICK

Oh, you don't know what you have done? You, brat! You're such a spoiled kid. That's it! I shall cut your pocket money as of today.

Tiny has tears in his eyes.

TINY

No! But Mom, I didn't do anything wrong.
This is unfair. Mom, please believe me.

ANNICK (Even more furious)

Shut up! You fool! What I'm going to do now! I can't move properly. It's all because of this mischievous drama!

TINY

But Mom, it's not my doing. Trust me. Mom,
this is unfair to me. I didn't do this.

TOMMY

Let it be, darling. He is only a kid.

ANNICK (Unable to control her anger)

I told you to shut up! Don't make me angrier. If not, there will be
more consequences, I am telling you…You better watch out, boy.

The lady blames and points a finger at her son.

ANNICK

Let us go home! I'll show you! You will be
punished even more for this act!

TINY (Tearfully)

Mom, please. Believe me, I didn't do it. Mom, please.

ANNICK

Stop it! Do you even realise that we are in a restaurant?

Vital is laughing soundlessly in his corner when suddenly he hears
someone.

Annick tries to untie the ribbon, but her are in vain.

ANNICK

Excuse me!

VITAL

Yes!

ANNICK

My mischievous son tied my dress to this chair, and
I can't untie it. Can you help me, please?

Vital tries untying her dress, but he willingly ties it even tighter.

VITAL

This is a very tight knot. I can't untie it.

ANNICK

Please do something.

VITAL

Wait. I have an idea.

Vital goes to the kitchen, takes a huge knife, and holds it behind him. Annick can see him smiling and running to her. He quickly puts it close to her.

VITAL

Here it is, madam!

The woman is terrified. She puts her hands at her heart fearfully and is breathing speedily. Tommy watches speechlessly

ANNICK

You fool…

Vital does not wait, and he runs to the kitchen again. This time, he brings a pair of scissors.

ANNICK

Oh my God!

VITAL

I fear this is the only way, or you won't be
able to leave. Allow me to help you!

ANNICK

Ok! And be careful!

Vital bends down and is thinking about how he can cut the ribbon.
He is about to cut the ribbon.

ANNICK

Be careful, please!

VITAL (Reassuringly)

Yes, ma'am. Don't worry! You're in safe hands.

Due to lack of concentration, he misses the piece tied to the chair, and
he ends up cutting the dress instead of the ribbon, but still, Annick is
finally able to move now.

ANNICK (Relieved)

Oh, thank you so much! You're so kind. I really appreciate it.

VITAL (Speaking very politely)

You're welcome, ma'am. It's my duty to help our customers.

TOMMY

See? He is a good person.

Pointing his finger at Vital

Meanwhile, the lady is touching her back. Suddenly, her expression
changes. She can touch herself but notices her dress is torn from the
back.

ANNICK

It was my favourite dress and also a birthday present
from my husband. And now it's all ruined.

Annick got so upset

ANNICK (Horrified)

'Oh my God, my beautiful new dress! Oh no, this can't be!'

Annick is almost in tears.

She looks at Vital angrily and shifts to another table.

VITAL

I was just trying to help.

Vital is fearless and pays no attention as he continues to accomplish his tasks. He goes behind the lady so as not to see her face. He removes the table mat and throws the waste without realizing they are falling on the woman. She stands up and moves a little.

VITAL

Oh! She is leaving.

ANNICK

Be careful!

Annick again takes her initial seat. Vital continues cleaning the table with a cloth. After he finishes, he puts the dirty cloth on the seat. In fact, without realising it, he accidentally puts the cloth on top of the lady's dress. He again takes it, cleans the table, dusts it, and taps it on the back chair. In reality, Vital is unaware that Annick is standing, and he is tapping her bum instead of the back chair.

ANNICK (Extremely Enraged)

'Excuse me! How dare you, you stupid waiter! Are you blind or what? You idiot! You are tapping my bum with your disgusting dirty cloth. I shall report you to the manager.'

She ferociously slaps Vital. Tommy reassures Annick

TOMMY

We are on a mission. We will fail. Keep quiet!

ANNICK

Shut up! You Stupid!

Vital takes the cloth and puts it inside a woman's bra who is sitting nearby.

BOTH LADIES (Angrily)

We will immediately report you to the manager.

They go and report Vital to the manager. Vital takes all the things and goes to the store. He throws the waste in the bin. He is so tired and revengeful that he has no idea how to escape from work. Angrily, he takes the bin and throws it by the window. Accidentally, it falls on Annick outside.

ANNICK

'Ahhhhhhhh…'

TOMMY (Enraged)

I will teach this stupid asshole a lesson!

The latter sees a man running furiously towards him. Vital runs away. Tommy chases Vital in the restaurant. Vital plays and mocks him.

ANNICK

'Catch him! Be… Be… Beat him! He deserves it! That asshole!
He threw waste on me and ruined my favourite dress.'

The situation becomes chaotic and out of control inside the Green

Dragon restaurant. Vital runs around the lady. Tommy attempts to slap Vital, but he moves too rapidly. Tommy misses his target, and instead of Vital, Annick receives the slap.

ANNICK

AIE.!!! It's him you must hit, poor idiot!

At the same time, a couple is entering the restaurant with a chocolate birthday cake. Vital snatches it and throws it on Tommy's face. The situation becomes more hilarious, with Tommy's face covered with chocolate mousse. Tommy is now very upset.

TOMMY

You rascal! Just wait. I'll show you who I am! You're a dead man now!

Vital runs to the store, trying to escape, but the man follows him. Suddenly, Vital is stuck in the store, and Tommy is just behind him. He is frightened and is looking at Tommy fixedly.

ANNICK

Catch him! What are you waiting for?

Vital finds plastic bins. He hurriedly takes a plastic bin and throws it on Tommy. The latter bows down, and Annick gets hurt instead. She was about to enter the store, but fell heavily backward at the entrance. Tommy turns back to see his wife. Quickly, Vital takes another bin and places it on Tommy's head.

TOMMY

You moron monkey! Take that off me! I can't see a thing!
Watch what I will do to you once I get this off my head!

Tommy is not able to remove it. He is walking like a complete, tight drunkard as he is not seeing anything. He is even more frustrated.

Tommy manages to get out of the restaurant. While walking, he accidentally trips over an iron pole and falls down.

ANNICK

Are you okay? I hope you're not hurt. Get up and don't spare that stupid waiter. Here, let me help you!'

She tries to remove the bin from Tommy's head but is having some difficulties doing so.

TOMMY

AHHH!!!! You are hurting me. AIE AIE!!!

Annick wrathfully runs after Vital. She sees an old crippled man walking slowly by the help of a stick. She swiftly pulls the stick to beat Vital, but the old fellow falls.

OLD MAN

No one has any respect for old people these days.

CONTINUES…

ENTER: MEERA, TOMMY AND GANG, RAM

Tommy removes a gun. Meera runs unremarkably away from the next door while Ram enters. Tommy notices Ram, shoots in the air, and holds Ram.

TOMMY (In a warning tone)

Calmly and quietly come with us! Don't force us to kill you here itself! You better come with us, you ant!

RAM

What if I refuse?

TOMMY

Don't try to act smart with us! Tonight, will be the last
night for you and that girl in the red dress! We have orders
to kill you both. The other day, you saved her, but tonight,
both of you shall die. We have come prepared this time.

Tommy and Ram are looking steadily at each other.

TOMMY

Put your hands behind your head and walk. Don't make
any noise. If not, we won't hesitate to shoot you.

RAM

Perhaps you haven't understood yet. I have come here to
teach you and your gang a lesson once and for all. Whereas
for me, you can't even harm me. So, don't even try!

Tommy gets impatient.

TOMMY

Then get ready to bear the consequences! You're a dead
man! Even your biceps can't save you today!

As soon as he says this, Ram jumps to give Tommy a blow. Tommy
bluntly falls down. Tommy's men arrive and surround Ram. Ram
quickly gives a punch and a kick to the men. He starts beating them
harshly. Tommy gets up and removes his gun. Luckily, Ram sees the
gun and runs to hide himself under the stairs. Tommy is firing one
after another while following Ram.

TOMMY (Tauntingly)

I told you, you are a dead man.

Ram manages to get outside the restaurant and runs. Tommy follows
him with a gun in his hands. Ram sees a crescent, and he quickly hides

behind it. He picks up a rock, puts it in his pocket, and climbs the tree like a monkey. Ram had to act fast to save his life.

As soon as Tommy arrives, Ram precisely throws the rock rapidly at Tommy. Tommy drops the gun as he cringes in pain.

TOMMY

Oops!

Ram swiftly jumps down on Tommy and beats him black and blue unceasingly. He only stops when Tommy is lying unconscious on the ground.

BACK TO SCENE

LOCATION: INSIDE THE GREEN DRAGON RESTAURANT

ENTER: ANDREW, YOUSEF, BOUNCERS, JENNIFER (ANDREW'S WIFE), AND MANAGER

Jennifer goes to the bouncers. They are trying to seek for some information.

JENNIFER

Have you seen a man with PEAU LAPAILLE,
avocado shorts, and a hibiscus flower shirt?

BOUNCERS (Sadly, thinking for a while)

Yes! If I am not mistaken. We have seen him, indeed. He's a
thief. It's been 30 minutes since he has left here. He looted
us. If we find him, we will badly teach him a lesson.

JENNIFER

'That man is my husband, and I am desperately looking for him
everywhere. I will be grateful if you guys could help me find him.'

The manager of the Green Dragon restaurant overhears the conversation between Andrew's wife and his bouncers at the main entrance of the restaurant. He rushes to meet the lady.

MANAGER TO STAFF (1)

This will be my chance to get compensation
for the food the guys had eaten.

Without wasting time, he rushes to meet her.

MANAGER

Oh, that man is your husband. Then you should pay for his bill.
After eating, he ran away. Now, it's your duty to foot the bill.

JENNIFER (sadly)

What? Okay, I'll pay for that.

She then pays for the bill.

MANAGER

Good. Thank you. I hope you will find your husband.

JENNIFER (Frustrated)

But me, the poor Jennifer, had not found her husband yet.

Afterwards, she keeps looking for him.

SCENE 17

EXT SHOT: IN THE STREET

LOCATION: ROYAL ROAD – IN THE HEART OF THE CITY

ENTER: MASTER, SUNIL, PRINCESS, PETER AND HIS SON, PAUL

Sunil sees a fortune teller named Master along the street. Master is wearing a long black magician attire. Master sees a princess going in her brand-new car. She is in a yellow Lamborghini.

MASTER

This is a golden opportunity to make money.

The car goes a few meters away.

MASTER (Happily)

Oh, the princess is going to S.P. Supermall! Ah ha, that's my chance. Let's go, Master! Let's make some money!

A man, Peter, comes along with his son, Paul.

PETER (Turning to Paul)

I have come to meet Master for his so-called astrology

skills. This Master is a genuine fortune teller who can
help predict good and interesting facts about YOU.

PETER (In a worried tone)

Master, that's my son, Paul. He is about to join school. I am
worried about his future. Will he perform well at school?
What about his grades? Can you please tell me his destiny?

MASTER (Smiling confidently)

'Good afternoon, Peter. First, you must put Rs100 on the table!'

PETER

'Wait, I'll come back! I'll bring my wife and the money!'

FADE TO BLACK

Sunil comes around. He is observing Master playing the deck of cards.
Master seems to be very good at it. Sunil is really keen to know what
happens next. He is observing very carefully. Master notices Sunil
watching him play the deck of cards.

MASTER

When it is hot, people should drink lemonade or alouda. When
it is cold, we drink tea or coffee. When we think our future is
not good, we see Master, and I'm here for your help. Why worry
when Master is here. What do you wish to know, my son?

SUNIL (Curious)

Tell me about my future!

MASTER

You are a good person, and you are very lucky as well. Put
Rs100 in my hand as I will tell you about your future now.

SUNIL

I do not have change. Someone has to give me
Rs400, and then I'll give you Rs500.

Master accepts and happily gives him the money, then looks at him

MASTER (Abruptly)

You are possessed by evil spirit! You are very <u>distressed,</u> my son.

SUNIL (Shocked)

How can you forecast that? Is it possible? Can you remove
the evil spirit? Please do something. I am scared.

MASTER

I'm a fortune teller! I can also predict! In twenty minutes, a
brand-new car, a yellow Lamborghini, will come, and if you
propose to that lady, she will become your life partner!

SUNIL (Skeptical)

Really? Are you sure?

MASTER

Of course, my son. I am a fortune teller.

Sunil is very curious.

SUNIL (To himself)

I think his words will come true

The princess passes by in her yellow Lamborghini. However, Sunil notices that the car does not stop.

MASTER (Feeling very proud)

Have you seen my forecast? So, what do you think
now? I trust my power, and you should, too.

SUNIL

But the princess didn't stop! How will I
propose to her if her car doesn't stop?

MASTER (Speaking very convincingly)

It is you who should have stopped the car! You are unfortunate,
my son! It is because of that evil spirit! See, I just proved
my point. It is very important that you remove this evil
spirit from your body; otherwise, your life is doomed.

SUNIL

Predict another thing!

MASTER (Sounding even more confident)

A man, a woman, and a child will arrive soon!

To Sunil's surprise, they really come. Master smiles and <u>then</u> laughs.

MASTER

Let me consult the first client and tell you!

Master is shuffling the deck of cards and talks hesitantly and quickly.
He taps the child with soft green leaves as if removing something from
the kid's body.

He speaks seemingly magic mantras to accompany his gestures.

MASTER

Hooo houm. Poom houm houm!!! Chal chal chal!!!

Master made more gestures.

MASTER

How do you feel, my son?

THE CHILD

I'm feeling well now!

The parent pays him and leaves him, thankfully. Seeing the action, Sunil is very <u>irritated</u>.

SUNIL

'Look at my prediction now. I am still waiting for
my turn. Check again and predict my future.'

MASTER

'An old red motorcycle dotted black will come
with two persons without proper breaks.'

They both wait, but the motorcycle never comes.

SUNIL (Smiling in a victory mode)

'Master, you are not more powerful than me. You don't
know my bravery. See! I can vanish if I wish.'

Sunil looks around, grabs the money from Master's hands, and pushes him aside.

SUNIL (To himself)

'Keep on waiting for your Rs400.

Sunil looks at the four red notes and laughs. He is so proud of himself and of his victory. He is walking away when Master is shouting at him from behind.

MASTER (Angrily)

You scoundrel, may you fall in the well, and
cockroaches eat you everywhere!

SUNIL

I know that will not happen. Your predictions are false.

CONTINUES....

Andrew and Yousef are still searching for Sunil on their motorbike. Andrew's pants are coming down again, so he stops his bike and gets ready to pull his pants.

Coincidentally, these two boys have reached the same street where Master and Sunil are arguing about the prediction. Andrew stares at Master. The police arrive.

MASTER (Talking to himself)

Oh God, It's the police again! My tricks won't
work now. Let's escape from here quickly.

Both parties go in opposite directions. Master packs his belongings, but the policemen appear.

POLICEMAN

Hey you! Stop! You are the fortune teller.

MASTER

No, no. I was just passing by.

POLICEMAN

What's under your arm? Oh, a folding table, mats, deck of cards,
candles. You are trying to fool us. There have been a lot of
complaints about you. In fact, you are fooling people and robbing
them. Now, follow us to the police station. Your game is over.

Master gets arrested.

Andrew and Yousef are still looking for Sunil. Both their phones ring at the same time. They jump like spring when they hear their wives' voices.

ANDREW

Darling, I'm still waiting for you at the shop X, dear.

YOUSEF (Talking to Andrew)

Sit and wait here while I'll move further to look for Sunil.

Sunil finds a spot. He goes and sleeps in a corner.

Yousef is still following and searching for Sunil on his motorbike. He is fed up and tired of searching for him.

Andrew is getting worried and stressed.

ANDREW

I am aware that my wife is waiting for me at the shop. I know she must be quite upset as she has been waiting for a long time.

He fears that she may call him again.

ANDREW

Maybe this time I will not have the courage to answer her call. I may not be able to come up with a good excuse.

Peter and his son, Paul, are coming.

PAUL

Dad, I want to pee!

FATHER

Go to that corner. No one is watching. Hurry up.

The child unbuttons his pant button and unknowingly pees on Sunil.
Sunil opens his eyes.

SUNIL (Irritated)

'Hey, what are you doing, boy? Yuck urine'

The boy gets scared and runs to his father.

Andrew's wife, Jennifer, comes. She moves forward in slow motion.
She is thinking of what her husband must be doing. Suddenly, she
meets Yousef's wife. Both of them have sticks in their hands, looking
for their husbands.

JENNIFER

What are you doing with a stick?

YOUSEF'S WIFE

I can return the question to you.

JENNIFER

So, you are also looking for your husband?

They begin to laugh.

YOUSEF'S WIFE

Let's look for them together. If we find one, we will
find the other one. They are like shirts and pants.

Sevdou finds Sunil. She happens to be Sunil's elder sister. She has been
looking for Sunil for a long time. Luckily, she finds him before anyone
else does. Sevdou sees that his clothes are different, wet, and smelling
so bad. She becomes nervous.

SEVDOU

'Yuck… you are stinking as if a dog has pissed on you, and whose clothes have you worn? Remove these clothes and throw them from this house; otherwise, I'll bring you to Dr Fousad. Do you know since when we have been searching for you? Tomorrow, you come with me to meet Dr Fousad.'

Sunil goes to a corner and hides the wallet and the cellular phone. Sevdou again knocks against him.

SEVDOU (Irritated & Annoyed)

Your bad odour will make people go into a coma.
Throw these clothes as soon as possible.

SUNIL

Yes, sister, I will throw it.

Sunil throws the clothes one by one.

Unknowingly, the clothes fall on Andrew.

ANDREW

Ohhhhh! Finally good clothes. Thank you, God.

Andrew is wearing the clothes one by one.

Andrew receives a message on his phone from Ajay.

PHONE SCREEN

You have won a race!

With style, Sunil throws the hat, which falls on his head.

ANDREW (happily)
Thank you, bro!

Yousef comes and listens attentively and becomes happier. They ride away.

Sevdou comes back and finds Sunil bare naked.

SEVDOU

I am fed up with your behaviour, Sunil.

She kicks him with her left leg.

SEVDOU (Shouting)

'Oh! You donkey! You are naked! Huff...f...f! Your hairy legs…! You are like a monkey! Wear clean clothes once and for all. How many times do I need to tell you to get properly dressed? Tomorrow, we both have to go to that doctor.'

She looks at her own dress and then looks at Sunil.

SEVDOU

Wear mine!

SUNIL

What? Which one? The hidden leggings… or your skirt?

SEVDOU

My legging is too thin. Please, Sunil, wear my jacket!

Sunil wears his sister's clothes. He looks at himself and blinks his eyes several times. He feels ashamed of himself. He is walking like a girl.

SEVDOU

You are a crazy person! Hold my purse! You deserve this!

SUNIL

You make me look like a girl.

SEVDOU

You deserve it.

He hides the wallet and mobile phone every time.

Later, Yousef and Andrew are hit by a car. It turned out to be the car of that princess, the yellow Lamborghini.

At the same time, Vital is coming in their direction and sees them. Having seen the clothes of Sunil

VITAL

Oh! My God! It is Sunil.

Vital instantly phones the manager of the restaurant.

VITAL (To the Manager)

Sunil met with an accident, and his figure has been deformed, but a lady, Jennifer, confirms it is her husband.

VITAL (To the manager)

It's strange. His body size also has changed. How is that possible?

BACK TO SCENE

YOUSEF'S WIFE

Oh my God! What has happened?

The ladies hold them tightly and drag them to their place while discussing.

CONTINUE

Sunil is awkwardly sitting at the bus stop with Sevdou. He feels so embarrassed that he is wearing his sister's skirt. He is checking here and there to see if anyone is looking at him. He secretly glances at the mobile (DON).

SUNIL (Talking to himself)

Hmm, how lucky, it's a new one. Samsung A72 is the
latest on the market and the most expensive.

He sees Felix's photo with gangs on the cell phone. He sees a second photo of Felix pointing a gun. Sevdou passes beside Sunil's room. Sunil is frightened.

FLASHBACK

He is shot by Felix.

He is shaven like spring. Sevdou notices the mobile phone and wallet when Sunil is lying on the floor.

SEVDOU (Screaming)

'Whose mobile phone is this? Wallet! Whose
wallet is this? Who does it belong to?'

Sevdou is completely furious and can't believe her eyes. She distraught with Sunil.

SEVDOU

I guess that you must have stolen these belongings.

She checks her wallet and finds the money. Sunil appears to be unconscious.

SEVDOU

Wake up! This time, they won't take you to Dr. Fousad but
to jail. Do you realise what you have done? This is a crime.
That person must be looking for his stuff like mad.

Sunil gets up and appears indifferent, as if he knows nothing. Sunil reacts as if he has lost his memory.

SUNIL

What are you talking about?

She shows him the mobile phone and the wallet.

SEVDOU

From where did you get this wallet and mobile phone? Who do they belong to?

SUNIL

'I don't know. This is a nice wallet. Whose wallet is it?'

SEVDOU

Do not irritate me more.

She hits Sunil, but he pretends to be innocent.

SUNIL (insisting)

It's my wallet!

Sevdou takes her phone and calls Ziko, Sunil's brother-in-law.

SEVDOU

'Hello, Ziko. Sunil has become a thief now. He has stolen somebody's wallet and mobile phone and is pretending to be innocent. It's such a huge crime. Please come immediately!'

Ziko arrives. Sunil is now quivering and is silent. Ziko is very angry with him.

ZIKO (Furiously)

Okay, Sunil. If you don't tell me on the spot to whom this wallet belongs, you will get into big trouble with me. Understand?

SUNIL

It belongs to a drunkard. He is not worth it.

ZIKO

He is worth it or not. That's not your problem. Just show us where he lives. We are going to return it to him.

Ziko takes Sunil by his collar, and Sevdou comes along with them.

Sunil talks by sign.

ZIKO (To Sunil)

Go and show me where that drunkard lives? Right away, Sunil! Come on! We are both very upset with you due to your misbehaviour. You crossed all your limits by stealing from people.

SEVDOU

Once we have returned this wallet and mobile phone to their original owner, you will be officially grounded for months. You won't be allowed to leave the house, that's it!

ZIKO

Let's go to the drunkard's house.

SEVDOU (Orders Sunil)

Remain silent, Sunil, and in the meantime, we shall return the drunkard's wallet and mobile phone.

Sunil listens obediently and waits at the main entrance of Felix's house.

Sevdou holds Felix's mobile phone and wallet. At the same time, the phone rings. Sevdou answers the call.

SEVDOU (Speaking Politely)

Hello, yes. Who is it, please?

DON (In a threatening tone)

Return the mobile phone, or else I'll kill you.

SEVDOU (Keeping Calm)

We are searching for you to return your belongings.

DON

'Okay, so meet me at Ramphul's hardware store.'

They both agree to meet at the spot Felix chose.

SEVDOU

No problem, we will be there in 10 minutes.

Sevdou hangs up.

SUNIL (Admittedly)

The mobile phone is for someone else, and the
wallet belongs to another person.

SEVDOU

You just remain quiet, or else we'll lock you in the prison.

Sunil remains silent. At the same time, the Felix's wife, Lily, comes out of the house and finds Felix tied with a rope up a tree. She has worn a sexy top and a cute skirt. Sunil looks at her while she is walking.

It's been only 10 minutes since she was here, and some people beat him and tied him to a tree. She sees them running away. At the same time, Sunil sees the woman, and he starts dreaming.

SUNIL (To Lily)

Now I know who the criminal is.

Sunil thinks that it was the man who was following them. Ziko takes out his mobile phone and calls the police.

ZIKO

Hello sir, quickly come to Ramphul's hardware store. We badly need your help over here. We also need some protection.

Sevdou and Sunil go out of the drunkard's yard.

SEVDOU (Giving instructions to Sunil)

Go and return the mobile phone to its rightful owner.
Also, don't forget to apologise to the man for stealing his
mobile phone. Apologise sincerely so that he doesn't take
any action against you. Say that you are very sorry.

Sevdou and Sunil walk quickly along the road. Suddenly, Sunil stops right in his tracks. He looks at Sevdou as if he finally understood one thing.

SUNIL (To Sevdou)

I doubt the man who was following us.

Sevdou looks at Sunil in astonishment.

Sevdou calls the Police.

SEVDOU

Hello sir, I'm Sevdou, and I know who the suspect is. Please come quickly to Ramphul's hardware store. It's urgent!

Sevdou and Sunil continue to walk. They stop walking as soon as they reach Ramphul's hardware shop. At the same time, the police arrive. Sunil searches for the man. At last, he finds Don standing.

SUNIL TO POLICE

There he is!

SCENE 18

EXT SHOT: IN THE STREET

ENTER: RAJ, SUNIL, MAD MAN, POLICE WOMAN, FELIX, CAR DRIVER

Sunil is walking in the street, and all of a sudden, he sees Raj.

SUNIL

I should run away

But Sunil stops. Raj appears to have been beaten by someone.

RAJ

Ah…..Oh my God… Please, help me! It hurts so much.
I badly need help. Please, help me, anyone.

Sunil looks at him elegantly and changes his voice in style. He coughs several times and approaches Raj.

SUNIL (In lady's voice)

Do you need any help, Sir?

RAJ

Yes, please, give me my glasses and, if possible, take me to the hospital. I would be incredibly grateful if you could help me, lady. I have been wandering in the streets for quite a while now. It is also getting dark, and I have not been able to find help yet! Could you take me to the hospital urgently, please?

SUNIL (In a female voice)

Sure, sir, but do you have money to pay for the taxi?

Due to the dark, Raj cannot identify Sunil and mistakes him for a lady.

Raj is in great pain, and is suffering a lot. He has been beated black and blue. Sunil searches for a taxi and tries to get a lift from somebody, yet no cars stop.

SUNIL (Desperately)

Lift, please!

Sunil touches Raj to lift him up. Raj screams in agony, unable to bear the pain.

RAJ (Yelling in pain)

Don't touch me; it's painful everywhere.

Sunil lets go of Raj's body.

SUNIL

Okay! Okay! I am not going to touch you if it hurts that much.

Sunil sees Raj's glasses. Sunil kicks it and looks at him laughingly. A car is coming. Sunil asks the car to stop. Unfortunately, it drives away. Sunil looks at Raj repeatedly. Sunil lies down on the street and acts injured.

SUNIL

This is the way I am asking the car to stop. I assume the car driver will understand that you need a lift.

RAJ (Astonished)

What happened? How come he is not hearing the sound
of a car and thought that he can stop hearing?

The car stops, and as soon as Sunil moves to the pavement, the car goes away.

SUNIL (To Raj)

Take out the money quickly!

Sunil searches in Raj's pockets and finds some purses. Sunil discovers that all of them are empty. Sunil is dumbfounded. He cannot believe his eyes.

SUNIL (Stunned)

You are a pickpocket! How come all these purses are
empty? Also, why would you steal empty purses? It
does not make any sense! Tell me about it!

RAJ (Taken Aback)

Wait, how come you know that I am a pickpocket?
Who told you about my real identity? I never said
anything about me being a pickpocket!

SUNIL (Talking to himself)

Shit! What did I say? I trapped myself by saying that to
him. Sunil, why can't you keep your mouth shut?

Sunil tries to repair his mistake.

Sunil looks at him fiercely. Raj also looks at him with hesitation, but he cannot see. Raj rubs his eyes. His vision is blurry.

RAJ

Your face seems familiar to me.

He blinks his eyes

RAJ

I think I know you! I have definitely seen you
somewhere! But where have I seen you?

Raj feels confused. However, Sunil avoids this confusion.

SUNIL

No, you don't know me! It's the first time I've
seen you! You're making a mistake.

Sunil lies even more to Raj.

SUNIL

I am new to this town anyway. So, how would you know me?

Moreover, Raj remembers the immense pain in his body. He again cries in pain. He then confides in Sunil about his unfortunate incident.

RAJ

Well, I have been beaten by a woman, and I
suspect that she is a police officer.

SUNIL

What a police officer! Why?

Sunil stops a car

SUNIL

Could you bring my friend to the hospital?

DRIVER

'Don't worry, just get in the car! I will take you to the hospital.'

Sunil climbs into the car, and to his surprise, he sees Felix, the millionaire. The car takes Raj on board, too. Sunil acts like a police officer with Raj.

SUNIL (In an authoritative tone)

Maybe there are only thieves there!

Raj looks everywhere. Now, he can see a bit.

RAJ

I have already reached my residential place. I'll get off here and walk the rest of the way. Thank you so much for the lift. I will myself go to the hospital tomorrow morning. I really appreciate the lift. Thank you, sir, for dropping me home. Goodnight.

As soon as the car stops, Raj opens the door and starts walking when he knocks against a big black lady in a police uniform.

RAJ

Oh shit! I am screwed! It's her again!

It is the same female police officer who had beaten him up after that bag incident on the beach. Raj starts shaking with fear. He is sweating, and his eyes are wide open out of shock.

POLICEWOMAN (Menacingly)

Well, well, well, who do we have here?

She recognizes Raj right on the spot. Raj is even more scared and trembles with fear. Felix hides his face.

POLICEWOMAN

So, remember me? I have been searching for you both for so long! Your gang also will soon be arrested! But you will have to come with me to the police station right now.

The lady holds Raj and takes him away with her to the police station.

POLICEWOMAN

All police stations have been alerted, and many police officers are on the streets to arrest the other goons.

Some police officers have stopped the car.

POLICE

We are enquiring about Felix and his gang.

They are showing him Felix's photo.

POLICE

There is a reward of Rs 50,000.

As soon as Sunil hears about the reward, he is excited and exposes Felix immediately.

SUNIL (To policeman)

Hello sir, yes, I know the man very well. Here you are sir, the thieves, and please arrest this man (Felix)! You can lock them now.

FLASHBACK

After a while, he sees Lily. "Dreaming…dancing".

LILY (To Felix)

I have told you so many times to stop doing these kinds of things.

FELIX

What kind of things, baby? We are enjoying life.

LILY

I can't live with you anymore; I am going
away forever! Goodbye Felix!'

CONTINUES….

ENTER: FELIX, LILY, SUNIL AND POLICE

Felix is taken behind the bars.

Sunil is walking arrogantly with Lily. One of the police officers calls out to Sunil.

POLICEMAN

Won't you take your reward?

SUNIL (Proudly)

Sure, I'll collect it later since Lily will be my wife and I have to collect my money from the SMS PARIAZ BOOKMAKER, too.
I am also planning for half of the amount to go to charity.

Sunil smiles and moves forward.

SCENE 19

LOCATION: PARK

ENTER: PEOPLE, ANNY, BILL, SUNIL, BOY AND GIRL

Sunil has a short glimpse of a girl wearing a white hat and pink dress kissing a boy on his lips.

Sunil shows this charade to a few people walking by.

SUNIL

Hey! Look at these two. Kissing in public.
Nowadays, teens have no respect.

Some people get angry when they figure out that they are teenagers and are heavily drunk. They see several cans of beer next to them.

Sunil takes a stroll in the park when he unexpectedly meets Bill.

SUNIL (To himself)

Hey Bill! You are the same man whom I had played that
trick with the left-over bottle from the bin at the seaside.

He meets Bill

SUNIL (In a happy tone)

Helloooo, Bill! How are you, mate?

Bill recognises Sunil. He smiles.

BILL

I am fine and hope that you are okay. You know, Sunil, I
have become a very serious and responsible person. I have not
consumed any liquor anymore. Anny changed me completely.

SUNIL

Really? Unbelievable!

BILL

You know, Anny is going to buy her wedding dress, and
she is waiting for me to make my choice. We are finally,
by the grace of Almighty, getting married soon

LOCATION: INSIDE THE WEDDING DRESS SHOP
ENTER ANNY

Anny has already chosen her dress and calls Bill, but her mobile battery
is low. She is waiting for Bill to help her decide which dress she should
pick.

ANNY

Oh no, I was supposed to call Bill and ask him about
his choice. Now, how will I make the final selection for
my wedding dress? What if Bill doesn't approve of dress
I have chosen? Oh God! What should I do now?

EXT PARK

SUNIL

Ha! Ha! Ha! She will not come. Trust me, I have just seen her
with a boy. She is enjoying her last day with her boyfriend.
If you don't believe me, ask a few of the people who were
sitting there. They were even kissing on the lips in public.

Bill really wants to investigate.

BILL

Have you seen a girl in a pink dress?

A person confess since Sunil gives them a sign.

SOMEONE

Yes. There in the park. Kissing with no respect.

Bill is so desperate that he rushes onto the highway, and Sunil follows
a few meters away.

SUNIL (Talking to himself)

It looks so funny. Just see the prank! He seems still drunk.

A vehicle suddenly swerves into Bill's path at a high speed, causing him
to abruptly alter his route in a desperate attempt to avoid it. Tragically,
his efforts prove futile as the car strikes him, sending him to the ground
with a force that would seal his fate.

Sunil, witnessing the horrific scene unfold right before his eyes, feels a
shock wave of horror ripple through him. Anny, who had just arrived
on the scene, stands frozen alongside Sunil, both of them among the
several onlookers to the dreadful accident.

The weight of what he has witnessed begins to press heavily on Sunil's shoulders. The guilt is slowly eating deep inside him, as though somehow, he might have been able to change the grim outcome.

SUNIL (Tearfully)

I know that I am the person responsible for Bill's
death. I just wanted to prank Bill this morning.

Sunil had thought it was just a harmless joke—nothing more than a bit of fun at Bill's expense. But he could never have anticipated the chain of events his prank would unleash. A catastrophe.

Each passing moment, his conscience gnawed at him fiercely, a relentless reminder of the irreversible mistake he had made. He sees is now that he would carry this burden for the rest of his life.

SUNIL (Talking to himself)

Oh God, please forgive me. I am the culprit. I
killed Bill. I deserve a punishment, God.

Sunil can't hold back his tears. He starts weeping incessantly while holding Anny.

SCENE 20

LOCATION: IN THE STREET

ENTER: SUNIL, MEERA AND RAM

Sunil spots Meera drawing the picture of Ram.

> SUNIL (Talking to himself)
>
> Oh! So, she is the lady Ram has been looking for so long! She is the one!

Sunil calls Ram.

> SUNIL (Happily)
>
> Hey dude, I've found your girlfriend! We met several times!

> RAM
>
> Okay, I'm coming! But if it's wrong this time, I will not spare you!

> SUNIL
>
> No, no. She is in front of my eyes. But come quick before she vanishes again.

Sunil looks at the drawing, admiring Ram's picture. He is in awe of Meera's talent as she continues drawing. Suddenly, he kneels down.

SUNIL

Oh God, really, this girl is Ram's girlfriend! Please unite
them! They are desperate without each other!

Without Sunil's knowledge, Meera moves her location. Ram arrives at
that very moment.

RAM

Where is she?

SUNIL

She is here! Look over there!

Sunil turns around and notices that Meera has disappeared.

SUNIL

Oh, where is she gone now? She was just here a few minutes back!

RAM

Gone? Really! All of a sudden! As soon as I am
coming! You think she is a phantom! You idiot, you
took me for a fool. Now, I will not spare you!

SUNIL

No, Ram, really she was here…

Sunil tries to argue with him to prove that he is telling the truth, but
Ram gives him a punch.

SUNIL

'It's the truth, dude! I'm not lying!'

Ram gives another punch to Sunil's belly.

SUNIL

Your girlfriend was really here a few minutes ago! Trust me, I am definitely not lying! She was right here drawing your picture.

As soon as Ram was about to give another punch, Sunil stops his hand and gives him a blow. Ram stumbles. They start beating each other, screaming.

SUNIL (Obtrusively)

'Aaahhhhhhhhhh!'

RAM (Loudly)

'Aaahhhhhhhh!'

Meera, who is still nearby, hears the noise.

MEERA

Who is that? I have to take a look!

Meera sees Ram, and she is mesmerised, and her eyes are full of tears. She can't believe how lucky she is that actually found Ram.

MEERA (Boldly)

Hey, stop it, you two!

Ram and Sunil stop. They look up and are shocked when they see Meera. They let go of each other's collar.

SUNIL (Joyfully)

What did I tell you!

Ram and Meera gaze and hug each other. Sunil looks at the drawing and silently leaves.

RAM (Loudly)

Hey dude, you were right!

SUNIL

I know. And now, be happy.

Sunil waves to them, as he walks away.

CUT TO:

SCENE 21

AFTER 2 WEEKS

LOCATION: NIGHT CLUB

ENTER: LILY, MEERA, RAM, SUNIL, BOY AND OTHER GIRLS

Lily and Meera are merry-making with Sunil and Ram in the discotheque. Sunil is dancing on the dance floor. But still, the ladies enjoy the atmosphere. He is offered bottles and bottles of liquor and is being well-treated. Sunil is sitting cozily on a large sofa with all these ladies in his arms and smiling.

SUNIL

But all this does not seem to fit me. I feel
that I am missing something.

He has pangs of conscience. He gets up and goes out. The realization dawns upon him like a cold wave. He feels his intoxicated spirit sobering up. He gently leaves the group, his decision firm. He casts one last glance at the spectacle of the club, then heads toward the exit.

As he steps out into the cool night, he feels the need to search for something more, something deeper.

SCENE 22

EXT SHOT

LOCATION: IN THE STREET, OUTSIDE THE NIGHTCLUB

SUNIL (Talking to himself)

Enjoy youth. You are not mine. I will not interfere in other people's lives and play pranks with anyone. I don't want to create more problems. I do not know if God will send a lady to me who I can trust and who will trust me. I am blaming myself strongly for what happened to Bill. I now think of different ways to fix everything. I know, Bill, that I can't bring you back from the dead, but still, if I could amend things or attempt to improve whatever is left behind after his death.

He is reprimanding himself.

SUNIL

I know that Bill and Anny won't forgive me, but I can at least go to them and apologize for my sins. I am going to fix everything. Oh God, please give me strength and courage to accomplish whatever I am going to do next!

Sunil then walks a long distance before finally reaching a grave. He sees the grave right in the middle of the cemetery. Under the moonlight, it was easy to spot it. It is covered with lovely and fresh flowers.

SUNIL (Crying)

Please do forgive me, Bill. I am the one responsible for your death. Please forgive me. It will appease my soul. I promise you that I will take all responsibilities of that dear one.

Sunil is running madly in the street.

SUNIL

I am coming, dear!

SCENE 23

ANNY'S HOME

ENTER SUNIL, ANNY AND ANNY'S MUM

He knocks at Anny's door.

Anny wakes up with a start. She looks up at her watch. It's almost three a.m.

Another knock on the door.

She gets out of the bed and heads for the door. She opens the door, and to her surprise, she finds Sunil standing at the doorstep.

SUNIL

'Hello dear!'

ANNY

What are you doing at my doorstep at 3 o'clock
in the morning?' Anything serious?

Tears are running from Sunil's eyes. He falls to his knees and bows down his head. Drops of tears are falling on the ground. He clears his throat and tries to speak, but his voice is broken.

SUNIL (Softly)

Sorry for what happened?

ANNY

What?

SUNIL

I know we just met recently. But I am attracted to you. I know
that you are the woman I am looking for. Believe me, my feelings
for you are very deep. I don't have a lot. But for you, I will work
every day. I will build an awesome future for you with these two
hands. You suffered a great loss. I don't pretend to replace Bill.
But I promise I will love you with every beat of my heart.

She is completely speechless.

Having heard somebody banging on her door, her old mother arrives
to meet Sunil. Anny moves away as she is unsure what to say. Sunil
tries to convince Anny.

Sunil gets up. He knows that Anny is shocked. He sees her mom.

He goes to Anny's mom and holds her hands.

SUNIL

Can I be Anny's close friend? Will you give your consent,
ma'am? Please do not refuse! I am begging, ma'am…

They all get very emotional.

Anny looks at her mother.

ANNY

I really don't know what to say.

ANNY'S MOTHER

Anny, my beloved daughter! You lost your future husband a few
weeks away, but please allow room for this guy in your heart.
It's 3 o'clock in the morning, and he is at your doorstep. This

something about his feelings for you. I know you are also suffering, and I can't see you suffer like that. It pains my heart to see my daughter cry. I won't allow you to suffer during your whole life. He will mend your heart, dear. Please give him a chance. His love and support will heal your heart and take away your pain.

ANNY (Hesitantly)

But mother…….

ANNY'S MOTHER

Believe me, my daughter, I am telling you by experience.

ANNY

Okay, mum. I will give it a chance.

Tears trickle down Sunil's cheeks.

SUNIL

Thank you. I won't deceive you.

She walks towards Sunil and wipes the tears from his cheeks. She places her hands into Sunil's.

ANNY'S MOTHER

God bless us.

SUNIL

Thank God for giving Anny to me.

Sunil hugs Anny

SUNIL

My life will never be the same again. Now, my life has a meaning.

THE END